Joey the Juggler

First published in 2008
by Wayland

This paperback edition published in 2009

Text copyright © Penny Dolan 2008
Illustration copyright © Bruno Robert 2008

Wayland
338 Euston Road
London NW1 3BH

Wayland Australia
Level 17/207 Kent Street
Sydney, NSW 2000

Series Editor: Louise John
Editor: Katie Powell
Cover design: Paul Cherrill
Design: D.R.ink
Consultant: Shirley Bickler

A CIP catalogue record for this book is available from the British Library.

ISBN 9780750255349 (hbk)
ISBN 9780750255387 (pbk)

Printed in China

Wayland is a division of Hachette Children's Books,
an Hachette Livre UK Company

www.hachettelivre.co.uk

Joey the Juggler

Written by Penny Dolan
Illustrated by Bruno Robert

WAYLAND

Joey was the juggler in Carlo's Circus.

He had a very small caravan.

So Joey had to try out his
tricks outside.

Up went the balls and down came the balls.

"Hoopla! Hoopla! HOOPLA!" he cried.

Up went the sticks and down came the sticks.

"Hoopla! Hoopla! HOOPLA!"

Up went the hoops and down came the hoops.

"Hoopla! Hoopla! HOOPLA!"
he cried.

"There is too much noise!"
shouted Madam Crystal.
"Too much HOOPLA!
Go somewhere else!"

But Joey had nowhere else to do his juggling.

He had to try out his
tricks outside!

Madam Crystal was coming
back from the shops.

She wanted to make
some pancakes.

Yap and Scrap, the circus
dogs, raced and chased
around her.

They raced in front of her feet.

Oops! Up went Madam Crystal's box of eggs...

...and down came
those eggs.

1, 2, 3, 4, 5, 6, 7, 8, 9, 10!

Joey caught every one
of them.

"Hoopla! Hoopla! HOOPLA!"
he cried.

Madam Crystal laughed.
"Thank you, Joey. You can
juggle here anytime!"

23

START READING is a series of highly enjoyable books for beginner readers. **The books have been carefully graded to match the Book Bands widely used in schools.** This enables readers to be sure they choose books that match their own reading ability.

Look out for the Band colour on the book in our Start Reading logo.

The Bands are:

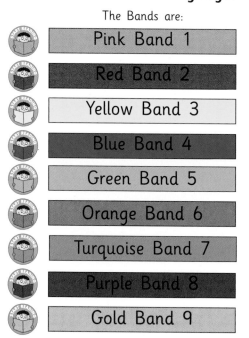

	Pink Band 1
	Red Band 2
	Yellow Band 3
	Blue Band 4
	Green Band 5
	Orange Band 6
	Turquoise Band 7
	Purple Band 8
	Gold Band 9

START READING books can be read independently or shared with an adult. They promote the enjoyment of reading through satisfying stories supported by fun illustrations.

Penny Dolan had great fun writing about Carlo's Circus, because she could pretend she was an expert juggler, brave trapeze artist, cheeky clown and an amazing elephant rider – even though she's definitely not!

Bruno Robert lives and works in Normandy, France, where he was born. He always wanted to draw and play with colours. When he is illustrating a story like this one, he likes to think of a bright and colourful world that is full of humour.